JUST'IN and the BIG FIGHT

BERNARD ASHLEY

Illustrated by Nick Ward

rbp

Ragged Bears Publishing

Also by Bernard Ashley
JUSTIN AND THE GRANDAD WAR

RAGGED BEARS
Published by Ragged Bears Publishing Ltd.
Unit 14A, Bennetts Field Industrial Estate,
Southgate Road,
Wincanton,
Somerset BA9 9DT, UK

This edition published 2009
1 3 5 7 9 10 8 6 4 2

A CIP catalogue record for this book is available from the
British Library

ISBN 978-1-85714-404-8

Printed in Poland

4

ONE

Justin was a good sleeper. As soon as his head hit the pillow, he was deep in the land of nod, his sweet face looking like an angel's. Justin Perfect. Who wasn't quite, but who thought he was.

It was his dad's favourite time of day. No more Justin answering back. No more Justin fighting with Miranda. No more reasons for neighbours to knock and file complaints. Mr Perfect would creep downstairs and pull a tab on a can to celebrate, every night of his life.

The down side was that Justin was always up with the sun, turning his room upside down and inside out with schemes and scams. He was forbidden to set foot outside his door before his dad was up – except to go to the lavatory – so, inside his room, bookshelves became bridges and bedclothes big tops; and if the cat strayed in she'd be trained for the circus until she got out of it by scratching.

But always at the first sound of a creak on the landing, the door would explode open as Justin hit the world.

Which made it all the more worrying on the day Justin didn't want to get up.

His father went past Justin's door and

had to check his watch. Not a sound. He showered and shaved and tiptoed back – still not a sound. He kissed the Gideons' Bible Justin had brought home from a holiday hotel and wondered if miracles happened these days.

Had the boy turned a corner? Was he into lying in, all of a sudden? Had he hit his teens early?

Or was he ill? Or had he climbed out

of his window and gone off to Disneyland Paris in the night?

Justin's dad bent to look through the keyhole, but he knew before he shut his spare eye that he was wasting his time. It was solid Blu-tack. He put one ear to the door and stuck his finger in the other; but all he could hear was the throb of his own blood on its daily gallop. He went in.

Justin was awake. He was in a knot of bedclothes that could have been mounted on a display board and sold to a sailor.

"Hello, son. You awake?"

"Do people sleep with their eyes open?"

"No –" Well, thought Justin's dad, at least the boy wasn't ill. "But, you're not up, are you … ?"

"Are my feet on the floor?"

This line of questioning was not getting Justin's dad too far.

"So what on earth's the matter with you?"

8

"Nothing."

"Get up then, get washed and dressed and get downstairs for your breakfast! It's Tuesday and you've got school today."

The boy somehow got himself out of his bedclothes.

"Are you sure you're all right?" Mr Perfect was a kindly man. He had been known to put his hand on his son's shoulder as if unafraid of being bitten; the lion-tamer touch.

"'Course I'm all right! What's up with you?"

"Nothing that a change of address

wouldn't cure," Mr Perfect said, and went to get into his overalls for a day at the greasy end of someone's car. Engines – now they were something he *did* understand.

Breakfast at the Perfects was like a picnic in a gorsebush: one wrong move and the prickles got you.

Normally for Justin it was half a packet of cornflakes and a litre of milk before the toast and peanut butter were attacked. Like any army expected to win the day, Justin marched on his stomach – which is why Mrs de Sousa, his teacher, who started with lemon tea and half a peach, never stood a chance.

But today, Justin picked at a dry cornflake or two – and on anyone foolish enough to comment.

"Lost your appetite?" his mother wanted to know.

"I can be *not hungry,* can't I? Don't have to shovel it in like *her*!" "Her" being Miranda, sitting up next to him on a stool.

"I expect he's in love," Miranda came back, with her sweetness-and-light face on; full knowing she might as well have rolled a grenade along the breakfast counter.

The box of "Start Your Day the Cornflakes Way" caught her on the head, its inside sprinkling her with morning goodness.

"Stupid *love*! Just cos you kiss all the boys … !"

"I do not!" The packet cracked back round Justin's ear.

"Stop it, you two!" Mrs Perfect yanked them both off their stools, put a brush in

Miranda's hand and a dustpan in Justin's. "Get that up! What a terrible waste of food!"

"Why should *I* brush?" Miranda moaned. "He's only got to hold the pan ..."

"Cos if I have the brush, you'll *be* in the pan!"

"Do you want me to get your father in?"

This was Mrs Perfect's ace, except she played it so often it didn't fool anyone. Mr Perfect was far too involved with a crankshaft to spare himself for United Nations stuff.

"He gets away with murder!" Miranda started brushing.

"I will get away with it, one day. An' no guesses who the victim's gonna be!"

Justin held the pan, a clever centimetre off the floor, where cornflakes wouldn't go in.

"*Mum!* There's something up with this boy, in a big way. Even he's not this bad most days."

Which was the moment the front doorbell went.

Justin stiffened: one second boy, the next second statue.

"It's only one of your little friends," Miranda said loftily.

Like something on a tombstone coming to life, his face the colour to go with it, Justin came up from his stoop and crept like a zombie to the door.

There was no face at the glass. It was someone shorter. He opened the door.

It was Tanya, from his class. As usual. Tanya, for whom Justin had his hair cut the latest way, cleaned his teeth, pinched his father's aftershave. Tanya, who came a close

second to football.

But today, his mouth was too dry even for "Hi!".

And so was hers. She stared at him, big-eyed and dramatic.

"You've got to do it," she said.

"Do what?" he asked. Knowing already.

He'd known all night, every second of all night.

"You've got to fight him. After school, Friday."

"Oh," said Justin. "Is that all? From the look on your face, I thought it was something serious."

And he turned back indoors to get his school things. But he was in such a state he kissed Miranda goodbye.

This *was* something serious.

TWO

Word was round the playground quicker than news of a Teachers' Training Day.

"Ty Power's gonna get Justin Perfect!"

" 'E's gonna beat in Tanya's boyfriend!"

"Friday, after school, in the hollows on the common. Big fight! Be there, son!"

"I've got Cubs …" one bemoaned.

"Miss it. *Leave*. Join again next week!"

Faces hadn't shown such glee since their birthdays. Tyrone Power was big, and in Year Six. Even Mr Anchor, the head, kept respect in his voice for Tyrone; and only the beautiful Miss Goody, his teacher, could make him smile. Justin was smaller, and in Year Four; but he was a scrapper. He didn't stand a chance against Tyrone, but it was going to be a fight worth watching. Years afterwards people would meet in the street and ask, *Were you there?*

19

Justin Perfect had fallen foul of Tanya's (very) big brother.

"What's it about?" Kojo asked Justin.

"Search me!"

"Yeah, they will. Search *for* you. An' they'll find little bits all over. A leg, a finger, half an ear ... Foxes'll set up at the hollows an' live off you all summer. They'll hold fox barbecues ..."

"Get lost! He might scare you, but he don't scare me."

"Is that why you're wetting yourself?"

And because Justin had to check that he wasn't, he was forced to give Kojo the low-down.

"It was *him*, that kid." Justin nodded across to where Clyde Smith was playing marbles. He was new, and that's where

Justin's problem had begun.

"Miss told us to look after him, make sure he knew where the lavs were, all that ..."

"I know." Kojo *was* in the same class.

"So, did *you* show him?"

"Nah."

"Not me, either. Soon as he said he wasn't into football I let him get on with it."

"Yeah."

"But Tanya did. She showed him where to get his dinner ticket an' all that ..." Now Justin wasn't sure how to say the next bit. Some things you could roll out of your mouth and you didn't have to think about them. But being soft on a girl wasn't one of them.

"I thought she was being too ... *nice* to him."

"Well, she *is* nice."

Justin sometimes wished everything was a game of football. In a game of football right now he'd have done a professional foul on Kojo for getting in his way. Everyone knew Tanya was nice; they also all knew she was *his* special friend. Which made all this worse.

"I told her she was only doing it cos he was a pretty boy."

It shut Kojo up, for a split second. "I'm not so bad looking myself," he said, "but she's never held my hand going to the lavs …"

"I *know*."

"So that's what you said?"

"Sort of." Did Kojo know how near he was to being used as practice for the fight?

"Them exact words?"

"No. Well, yes. No." Why couldn't Mrs de Sousa come out so that he could give her some cheek and get sent to the head. Anything to get away from this.

"I asked her, was she gonna marry him an' go on honeymoon? She didn't like that."

"Too right! That's well out of order!"

"I know that! An' then Tyrone says she's his sister, an' anyone who cuts up with her cuts up with him."

"Into little pieces …"

Which was back where they started. And before another word could be said, in came Tyrone through the gate.

The playground went dead quiet. Games

stopped. Talk held its breath. Heads twisted
to Tyrone, then round to Justin. Give them all
silly hats and sunglasses and it would have
been like the Centre Court at Wimbledon.

Big Ty himself came to the middle of the

playground and stopped. He looked around, pointed at Justin like the angel of death, didn't say a word, but smiled in a rubbing-his-hands sort of way; then he walked on over to some Year Sixes and got a cheer.

While all Kojo could do was clap Justin round the shoulders and say, "Glad it ain't me, son!"

THREE

Justin was different from other people. He was his own best friend and his own worst enemy, both at once. He had a slant on life which was *his* slant. And he always landed on his feet.

His was the first name teachers learned in the school, whether he was in their class or not. They never needed to ask if Justin was in the room. They knew. In Assembly, the first face Mr Anchor looked for, as they filed in, was Justin Perfect's. On one rare Justin-away Day the head had actually enjoyed talking to the school; got a laugh and milked it. The hand holding the hymn book had been firm.

Today, Justin was different, and Mrs de Sousa should have made more of him being in shock. It was a bonus from the gods which

wouldn't come to her again. She was halfway through her year with the boy in her class. The back of her bedroom door had a school year calendar on it with "days to go" about even with "days got through".

That morning she simply thought he was going down with something, and she thanked her lucky stars. Her horoscope had been right. *The overlap of Venus and Mercury means the sight of a silver lining.* When she had time, she decided to check his medical record to see what diseases he hadn't had, in the hope that he hadn't had anything. Meanwhile, at playtime, she sent out for cream cakes.

"But you had a birthday last month …" Mr Branston nibbled into a Viennese slice.

"Yes, but Justin Perfect's under the weather …"

"Heaven be praised!"

"Long may it continue!"

"Lock up the medicines!"

"He hasn't said a word all morning," Mrs de Sousa rejoiced. "Kept himself to himself, and his nose stuck into his work."

"Is he getting it right?"

"Who cares about *right*? He's being quiet."

There was talk of going to the pub at lunchtime, Mrs de Sousa treating. She couldn't stop smiling. Miss Goody, who was a new teacher this year, saw in her a woman she didn't recognize; at first, she thought Mrs de Sousa's daughter had popped in.

Teachers la-la'd as they rinsed their mugs. All at once, teaching seemed a worthwhile job to do.

But on the Wednesday, the world returned right side up. Justin Perfect was not letting anyone get him down, not even Tyrone Power, if he could help it.

He had never been to judo. The idea of standing in a line in white pyjamas, doing what some bloke told you, was not his scene. But he had heard about the judo system of awards. Kids in his class brought in certificates and got them read out in the hall by Mr Anchor – anything for a clap.

So in his mother's wardrobe he had found a scarf. It was an evening-dress scarf, bought for the Motor Engineers and Petrol Cashiers' Summer Ball at the Harvester. It still had its ticket and plastic tag on it. But it would do him a turn before it was needed next month.

He stuffed it in his pocket to get it out of the house, didn't show it to Tanya when she called for him. There was always the chance

Big Ty had changed his mind.

But no chance: Tyrone was going to turn Justin *Perfect* into Justin *Ruined*, he reckoned. And Tanya was *so* sorry she'd told him what Justin had said about Clyde.

"An' I can't be there to cheer you," she said. "I go faint when I see the colour of blood."

Justin dumped Tanya at the school gate and went into the outside lavatories, braving

the pong and the flies. Pulling a cubicle door shut on himself, he whipped out the black scarf and tied it round his waist, like a monk's belt. Coming out, he gave Kojo the slip and crept round by the wall to slide into the school and up to Mr Anchor's office.

The man was there, with a mug of tea

Branston

and a choccie biscuit, looking for letters he
might fancy opening.

"'Scuse me, sir."

"Yes?" Could that be the boy Perfect,
calling him *sir*?

"Look what I got rewarded."

"And what's that?"

"My black belt, judo."

"Eh?" Mr Anchor had looked away to check that it wasn't April the first; now he swung back so quickly he gave himself a hot crick in the neck. "You go to judo?"

Justin wasn't a liar. He was a truth bender.

"Black belt. Top award, the Grand Vizier said."

But he should have done his homework. *Grand Vizier?*

"What are you on about?"

"A clap in Assembly. You can pronounce it to everyone. 'Justin Perfect is now licensed to kill'."

"Really? Do you get a certificate to prove it?"

"*You* couldn't read it, it's written in Judo. I just brought the black belt to show you."

Mr Anchor put down his letters. It wasn't often he got this whiff of victory in his

nostrils. "May I touch the award, to say that I have touched a black belt?"

"I don't s'pose the Grand Vizier minds."

Mr Anchor buzzed through to the school secretary.

"Mrs Grossmith, could you step in, please?"

When the head asked that, it usually

meant he needed rescuing, so Mrs Grossmith stepped in, lively.

"Have *you* ever seen a judo black belt?" Mr Anchor wanted to know.

Mrs Grossmith hadn't. But now that she was present, Mr Anchor felt encouraged to untie the scarf from Justin's waist and hold it up for her to see.

" 'Dry clean only'," she read out from its label. And those other crucial words – " 'Dorothy Perkins'." The High Street shop.

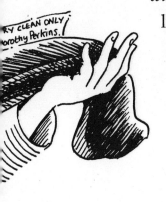

"They pass 'em on." Now Justin *was* inventing, if not outright lying. "It used to belong to this Dorothy Perkins, now it's mine." He tried to get it back. "After she left ..."

Mrs Grossmith laughed. Mr Anchor joined in, higher. "Nice try, Justin."

He turned to the secretary. "It's a shame to stop someone winning a bet ..."

But there were two losers. Justin, of course – and with the knock-on effect, Mrs de Sousa, who had to put up with his foul temper for the rest of Wednesday.

Wednesday.

Two days to go before the big fight – and no sign of it being called off.

FOUR

Justin liked cartoons. And Justin's parents liked him liking cartoons. Cartoon videos kept him quiet, and there wasn't a Disney release that they didn't get, hadn't had their names down for, weeks in advance.

One of his favourites was *Dumbo*. Which he had watched again and again and again. It hadn't been a waste of his time. Going home on the Wednesday he was anxious to talk to Tanya about it – but he had to wait for her usual buzz of Big Fight talk.

"I've never seen Ty so sharp on something," Tanya told him. "I keep saying you never meant what you said, but he won't take that. Just goes on saying 'revenge', all mean and growly."

Justin wanted to say he was surprised Tyrone could manage such a big word, but he

steered clear of even *thinking* about a further insult. One big fight was bad enough.

"You reckon he ought to fight me?"

"No! I told you, I go faint at the colour of –"

"Yeah, the colour of blood."

"Honest." She stroked his arm, turned it

into a hold of his hand, just for a few steps. It gave Justin a nice tingle round the back of his neck. It made breaking his big idea easier.

"Well, I've got a plan."

"What, for the fight …"

"No, for not having the fight."

"What's that?"

Justin stopped. When he had something important to say he always had to stop. Why should the world go on while he was changing it?

Tanya stopped too, which was handy.

"You ever seen *Dumbo*?"

"'Course."

"There's this bit, when the little mouse puts this idea in the ringmaster's ear. When the bloke's asleep. The mouse whispers in his ear what he's got to do. Like, as if it's a good idea coming to him in his dream."

"About Dumbo doing something better in the circus?"

"You got it. Well, tonight, you stay awake, right? Or put your alarm on for when Tyrone's asleep …"

"Yeah?"

"And when he's dreaming his dreams, you go in his room and whisper in his ear.

Don't fight Justin. Bad things will happen if you fight Justin. Something like that. Then he'll wake up in the morning and think he's been told it in the dream."

"Who by?"

"You, stupid."

"No, who by in his dream?"

"Oh." Justin walked on a bit. He talked

standing still, but he thought on the move. "God," he said.

Tanya didn't seem to like the sound of that.

"Or the angel of mercy, or someone."

"Could do," she said.

Another stop. "Do it for me? I mean, you did get me in this."

"I never. You said what you said first …"

"But all the same, you don't like the colour of blood, do you?"

"No." She walked on. "That's why I'm not gonna be there."

Which still didn't please Justin. Nor having to *plead* to get out of his fight. He pulled one of his Justin-isn't-happy faces, the one that got him extra sweets off aunties.

"OK," Tanya said suddenly.

"Only if you like ..."

"I like," she said. And she touched his hand and tingled him again.

Tanya thought she'd give it till twelve o'clock. Which wasn't going to be easy. She didn't have an alarm clock because Baby Sis was the alarm in their house, and you couldn't set Baby Sis to go off when she didn't want to. Or to stop when she did.

So Tanya had to keep herself awake till twelve. But that was easier planned than

48

done. She stayed up downstairs as long as her mum's patience lasted, then she went very quiet so as not to be noticed, and *got* noticed on the suspicion that she was up to something – which packed her off to bed. And in her bedroom, after a long play, she was forced in the end to get undressed and between the sheets. Then it was a bit of a think before she went under with *Girl* and a torch to keep her awake, and the next thing she was deep in her dreams.

When she woke up, the house was dead quiet, which was rare, so she knew it had to be the middle of the night. But she couldn't check, because she'd left her *Minnie Mouse* downstairs.

She knew what she'd got to do and say, though. She'd gone over the lines before she'd settled in with *Girl*.

Don't fight Justin Perfect. Bad things will happen if you fight Justin.

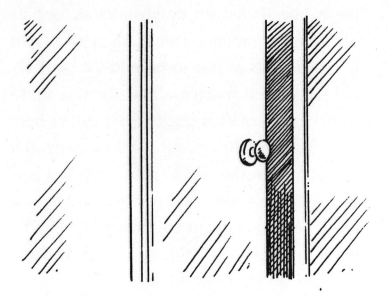

She said it over and over to herself in a dreamy voice and nearly went off to sleep again – but caught herself in time and crept out of her room and on to the landing.

It was spooky, out there alone, no lights on, her mum breathing heavily through the open door. That was a frightening sound on its own, like it was *not* her mum doing the noise, but some freaky spirit of the night.

Tanya wanted to cancel everything and

get back under her bedclothes.

But she didn't. She'd said she'd do it for Justin, so she would.

Tyrone's door was shut. It always was. *Brother Secret*, that was Tyrone. But she knew the turn of its handle; she went in there more than he ever knew – when he was out.

Tonight, though, he was in. He was a big lump in the bed, more like a hippo asleep under the clothes. She looked at him, sized him up, just hoped she could get at one of his ears.

Tiptoe, tiptoe, she went, across the ruck of his rug – no tripping, Tanya – and up to the side of his bed. Close. She could feel the warmth of him, smell the curl of his hair-gel. She listened hard for the sound of his breathing – but he must have been deeply asleep, because it was too soft to puff out a candle.

And there, thank you, *thank you*, was an ear – sticking up on top like something just *made* for secret messages in the night. Brilliant! Top wish! She'd have done more harm than good whispering up his nose.

She inched in, slid one hand under his pillow, took her weight on it and balanced herself so she could lean right over him. His ear was cocked up like a little microphone, all set at the right height; it seemed to be asking her to say, "Testing, testing, one, two,

53

three, four, five ..." But she didn't; she got right to the point. Do it while the ear's on top, she told herself.

This fight with Justin ... She growled it out low, because with the shakes that had suddenly come she hadn't got the breath for a whisper.

Tyrone moved a fraction: sort of, *receiving, receiving, loud and clear ...*

Don't fight Justin, bad things will happen if you fight Justin Perfect.

And Tyrone, eyes tight, arms floppy, rolled over and made a smacking sound with his mouth and gave a little snore.

The sort of noises which said his dreaming muscles had understood, like the ringmaster in *Dumbo*.

Done it! She'd done it! She'd got the

message in. Now, for Justin's sake, she could only hope that it worked like it had in the film.

She slid her hand out from under the pillow, stood up and turned, tiptoed back across the rug, reached a hand out for the doorknob.

And Tyrone spoke, in a voice all deep and monotonous, something from the trance of sleep.

Shut the door as you go out, sis.

FIVE

Justin heard the bad news and had a go at Tanya for trying. Now that it hadn't worked, couldn't she see what a stupid idea it had been?

"I was only joking – now he'll think I'm scared of him."

"But you are scared of him."

"Who says?"

"Your shaking says."

Which was a view of himself Justin hadn't wanted to give to the world.

"But I think I can save you," she went on. "I know his ticklish spot."

"What?"

"When we have fights indoors, romps with our dad, you can always get Ty with a tickle. He can't fight when he's being tickled. He wriggles all over and squeaks like a prawn. Gives in, easy-peasy."

"Does he?" This was interesting news to Justin, to someone who'd be having the romp of all romps with Tyrone. "And

where is this tickle place?" Justin hoped it wasn't anywhere out of bounds to a stranger.

"His neck. Under here." Tanya put up a hand and tickled Justin under his chin; which didn't do a lot to him. Not tickle-wise.

"Does it work every time."

"Dead cert."

"So if I make him miss with his first punch –" Even *saying* a word like "punch" hurt Justin – "I can get in and pretend to wrestle, and go for his tickle place."

"Sure-fire," Tanya said. But not really sounding sure-fire enough to have Justin giving out any tickets to the big event.

He needed a back-up. So he tried to get ill. Around the playground he looked out every kid who'd got the snuffles, or what could be spots; he went over to them and put his arm round them like an old pal, breathing

in hard to catch their germs. "Wotcher!" he said, as if he were a one-man welcome-to-school committee.

"Get off, you doz!" a Year Six hay-fever case sneezed – while Justin did a dive to breathe it in.

But as the day went on he knew he wasn't going to get ill in time. The same as with eggs and small babies, germs had to incubate. He also knew he couldn't pull the ill stunt with his mum and dad, not without proof. They'd had all that before, and it never worked.

"When they send you home in an ambulance you can have the rest of the day on the settee," his mum always said. "Then, we'll see …"

He needed another back-up. So, having checked that greens had iron in them, he ate a double helping on Thursday night, and went out to do a few press-ups on the grass.

At bedtime he got the nearest he could to asking for help.

"Say you got in a fight …" he said to his dad.

Mr Perfect stopped at the door as if a drugged dart had hit him.

"An' he was a big bloke …"

"Ye-s …"

"How would you win?"

Mr Perfect looked at the lad. What *had* he been watching? This didn't sound like research for a school project.

"It depends," he said. "If I was in a fight defending you or your mum or Miranda, I'd stand and slug it out – and kick him, knee him, grab hold of his hair, use every trick in the book …"

Justin wondered where he could get hold of this book. It'd be more use than *My First Encyclopedia*.

"What about tickling him?"

The boy was definitely off the short list for Brain of Britain, Mr Perfect thought.

"Unlikely." But now was the time for real fatherly advice. "But if I wasn't defending you, son, if it was just myself, if some bozo had picked a fight in a pub, or something …"

"Yeah?" This was getting more like it.

"And he was bigger than me, or had some mates …"

63

Spot on, this was. "Yeah?" Justin would have reached for paper and a pen: except he didn't have any paper, and he didn't have a pen.

"I'd run. Run like mad. The best way to win a fight, boy, is not to have it. Out of the door and up the street. Two good feet, they're your best weapons."

"Oh." If that was in the book of fighting tricks, they could keep it.

"Does that answer your question?"

But Mr Perfect would never know. Justin was off, back downstairs to see if his mum had a tin of spinach in the cupboard: it always worked for Popeye. Because he wasn't going to run from Tyrone, he was going to have to

fight him. Justin wasn't defending his loved ones like his dad talked about, not his mum or the cat or Tanya – but he *was* defending the name of Justin Perfect.

SIX

On the Friday morning Justin woke to a clear, new day. He came out of his dreams, had a split second of feeling normal, and – wallop! – smack into real life.

Today was the day when he was going to fight Tyrone Power. Today was the day when Justin Perfect would change, outside and in. This was the last morning of the old J.P.

He went over and looked in the mirror, finding a clear space between the faded "Well done" stickers which a student teacher had given him, years ago in the Infants, to keep him quiet.

He looked at his nose. Not a bad little job, fairly straight, it sniffed all right, did what was asked of it. But the question was, what would it look like this time tomorrow? Not

the same, that was for sure. He bent it to
one side, he flattened it. "Wotcher, Tanya,"
he said, all thick and nasal, to test what a
broken snout sounded like.

He looked at his ears. Nice little items,
not over large or flappy, they picked up
what was said, when he wanted to hear it.
He squashed one over, to see what he could

hear with a cauliflower ear. "Morning," he said; but although he could hear that all right, he knew it was from the inside, so he couldn't really go by that. But he knew he'd be finding out tomorrow.

He looked at his eyes. Not a bad pair. They matched, and he could see what he needed to see. And all right for winking, at parties and that. He closed one, pictured it blackened and closed up. Because this was how it would be tomorrow.

He looked at his mouth. He smiled into the mirror. Two rows of teeth, and two second teeth top front, even-steven. But he wouldn't have them both tomorrow. He put his tongue up over one, made it look like gum. And he shuddered at what he saw: the Justin Perfect smile, Day-after-the-Fight version.

He closed an eye, squashed an ear, flattened his nose, curled his tongue. "Hello, Tanya," he mumbled to the mirror.

"Hello, Quasimodo," said Miranda, who had come into his room looking for the cat. "You seeing what you'll look like after the fight?"

"NO!"

But, worse than catching him at the mirror, she knew! She was in Year Six, so she knew;

Justin hadn't thought of that.

"I'm practising what *he'll* look like."

"Not!"

For a second, for just a second, Justin thought about it. What about Miranda – what about using her being in Year Six to get to Ty Power? What about getting her to call him off?

Rubbish! What a wheelie-bin idea! He could sink pretty low, but there was no way he was asking horrible Miranda to do him any favours.

"Get out!" he said. "Or I'll start practising on you!"

"Oh, help," said Miranda. And she walked away, never knowing how near she came to having a full fish tank on her head to wear to school.

If the school had been buzzing on the Tuesday, it was roaring on the Friday. Attendance was at an all-time record high. Children had come in from their sickbeds to be there. Clinic appointments had been cancelled. A family due to leave had had their moving day put back. Mr Anchor was tempted to phone the local paper and claim

a community award.

And, against all the betting, Justin was there as well as Tyrone.

Coming into the playground Justin did his usual quick check, the one which had made his stomach go funny all week. Was Ty Power there, or had he by some miracle gone down with something good and serious?

But he was there, leaning against the

doorway of the boys' lavs. And, as soon as Tanya had run off to get into a game of football, he was crooking his finger to get Justin to go over to him.

Justin looked over his shoulder. *Him?*

"He's gonna do you *now*!" Kojo said in his throat. The sort of right hand man you could do without.

But in a weird way Justin hoped Big Ty

would do him now. It'd get it over with, wouldn't it? He wouldn't have the whole day to wait. And here in the playground with all the teachers inside, the shouts of "Fight! Fight! Fight!" would soon bring someone out to stop it. And that would be that. Justice would be done. Revenge taken. The end of the story.

So Justin went over, like a gladiator to the lion.

"Yeah?" He almost wanted to say, *sir*.

But he stopped short of that, and he stopped short of Tyrone's reach – while kids who had come too close were being sent scuttling with a look from the big boy, a powerful, fierce look that fried their cheeks.

"This fight," Tyrone said.

"Oh, yeah? Is that today?" Justin glanced at the watch he hadn't got on his wrist.

"End of the world's at four o'clock."

"Knew there was something. Where's it

gonna be? Didn't bring my diary ..."

It was the hollows on the common. The map of the quickest route from there to hospital was tattooed on Justin's heart.

"What I was gonna say ..." Tyrone went on.

Justin had never wanted to know what someone was going to say so much in all his life.

"I ain't gonna paste you just for this lot to dribble over. This is private, you an' me, right?"

It could be as private as Tyrone liked. It could be so private it never happened ...

Justin nodded.

"So while they're all jiving over the common to see your blood an' guts go spurting, you an' me, we'll settle it private. Behind the kitchen, over there ..."

Justin had the face of something carved in stone over a cathedral door. A martyr in shock. And, like one of those long-gone martyrs, no words would come any more.

"Cooks go 'ome three o'clock," Tyrone said. "No one won't see us, man."

Justin wanted to ask about the emergency services, but he left it.

"Right?"

Justin nodded; and even that hurt his neck.

"If anyone comes, it means *you've* told 'em – an' that's one more finger comes off! Right?"

Justin turned away and walked back to Kojo. Right.

"What did he want?" Kojo asked.

Justin couldn't help it. Justin would always be Justin. "Only wanted me to let him off," he said.

"Yeah?"

"Some chance! No way, son. Not now. I told him, he's all mouth, so he's gonna have his talk rammed down his throat with his teeth."

And just for a second Kojo believed him.

SEVEN

The school emptied fast on Friday afternoons, Mr Anchor's Robin Reliant usually leading the rush. But today the kids who fancied seeing the sight of blood made sure they beat him to it. The school gate could have done with football police on horses. Off they all crowded to the hollows on the common, where one of the little dells would make a natural arena. It was just the way the bloodthirsty Romans would have liked it.

Some didn't go. None of the adults, of course – although earlier in the week Justin *had* tried to interest Mrs de Sousa in an after-school nature ramble on the Friday. But, tart as lemon juice, she'd told him she'd be round at the doctor's.

Tanya didn't go. She'd done her best to make Justin feel good, reminded him about

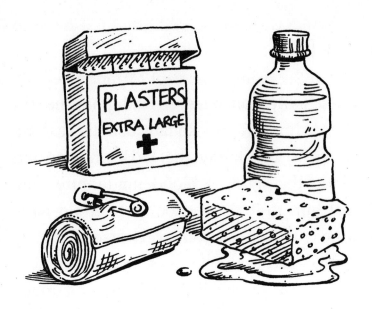

Ty's ticklish spot; but when she'd gone on again about how giddy she went at the colour of blood, he'd told her to get off out of it, quick.

Kojo went though. He wanted to go with Justin, to "hold his coat" for him. He'd borrowed an art sponge and brought a bottle of water, a packet of plasters and a sling – a real morale booster. But Justin said he'd meet him over there; told him he wanted to hype himself up on his own.

Year Six went, all except Miranda Perfect. She wouldn't wish this pasting on her worst enemy – which Justin was – so she took herself straight home. But the rest of Big Ty's class marched themselves out of the gate chanting, "Ty-rone, Ty-rone, Ty-*rone*!" Someone had made a banner, "Tyrone IS the Power!"

Obeying orders, Justin didn't go. He hung about in his classroom as it all went quiet. He mooched up and down on glass legs, and looked at things he'd probably never see again. With a bone-dust mouth, he said goodbye to the goldfish.

"Cheers, mate, we've had some good times together ..."

His insides felt as if the workings had moved out and a nest of rats moved in.

A cleaner came into the room and knocked a tower of chairs off a table with the careless end of her broom. At the sudden sound of it Justin nearly went through the window, and saved Tyrone the bother.

"Oi, son, shouldn't you be off 'ome?"

Yes, he should. Dear Mum, if only he could!

With a tick like the crack of an axe on a block, the classroom clock finally said it was time to go.

So Justin went, to face his doom behind the kitchen. He had to think about how to put one foot in front of the other – but he still managed a last push at a table to bring the chairs clattering down again. Well, it could

be some time before he felt well enough to be a pain.

To say there was no one behind the kitchen would be wrong. There was no one else behind the kitchen; but Tyrone Power was. He was leaning with his back against a wall looking like someone ready to push off and

sort out Justin in a mega way.

Justin came round the corner and stood on the small triangle of thatchy grass facing Tyrone, his hands bunched for punching and his boots – he'd chosen boots instead of trainers today – set for kicking. He stared the bigger boy in the eye, and he saw with a clunk of his heart that Tyrone was wearing a high-neck shirt, tight buttoned, which Justin hadn't noticed that morning.

So the tickling trick was off his battle plan.

All the same, Justin stood his ground as Tyrone stared.

"Come on, then!" One of them had to

break the silence. Justin beckoned Tyrone on like someone parking a car.

And suddenly Tyrone came on – so fast that before Justin could even think about taking a swing, he'd pushed him on to the grass and was sitting on him with a *thunk* which put his middle up his chest and into his throat. Tyrone pinned him to the grass with two hands, no chance to move.

"Right, Perfect –" he said with a scowl – "I'm gonna – "

He was gonna knock the dust off him. Justin stared helplessly into the boy's fierce eyes. So here it came after all the wait, now for the revenge pasting, now for the alteration of his face.

"I'm gonna let you off."

Justin would have blinked in disbelief, if he could have risked losing his focus.

"You've bled inside this week, haven't you, son? You've been scared *skinless*."

"Eh? Not on your life …" Justin managed – who was his own worst enemy, beyond doubt.

"Nah, I reckon you've hurt more inside than you would out, boy."

"Definitely not." The brave fool.

"An' you've learned your lesson about bad mouthing my family, right?"

Well, he had that. But Tyrone, in his letting off, had relaxed the pressure just a

touch. And Justin, streetwise supreme in his own fighting weight, sensing his chance, suddenly heaved with his belly and pushed down with his feet – and up went Tyrone, and over sideways, while Justin jumped to his feet and took up a kill-me-or-be-killed position.

"Hah!" he shouted.

"I told you, Perfect …" Tyrone dusted his hands and faced him again, ready and able

without a shadow of doubt to be the one doing the killing.

Justin stared at him. "OK," he said, "I'm sorry about what I said to Tanya. She knows all that." His heart was thumping itself out of his shirt already. He knew he was going to get beaten in, but he'd never bottled out of a fight in his life. "I said I'd fight you about it, an' I'll fight you."

"You're gonna get skinned alive."

"Then you can make a nice handbag out of me." Justin was going to add "for yourself" but he stopped short of mindless aggravation.

"You sorry, are you?"

"I said I was. But that don't make –"

"Then I ain't fighting *you*." Tyrone dropped his guard, stood showing his palms like an envoy of peace. He reached out a hand for a shake, really non-threatening.

"Mates? If you're sorry, we're mates."

Justin swallowed. What it was he didn't know, it tasted like blood, but it couldn't be, there hadn't been any of that.

"Mates," he said. And he shook Tyrone's hand, with just his animal instinct ready for a surprise attack.

But the surprise wasn't in an attack. It was in what Tyrone said – his final blessing.

"You're a brave little beggar, Perfect. All that lot has gone like a herd of sheep to see you get kicked in – they'd all run a mile from me, but you come here to take it."

Not often was Justin stuck for a word; but he couldn't dig out so much as a clear of the throat.

"Yeah, boy," Ty went on, "I'm proud of you. I reckon you've got every right to be Tanya's friend."

And he gave him a hug of respect, before the two of them walked off, their arms looped round each other's shoulders; like a couple of blood brothers.